THE SUPERSTAR

KICK!

THE SUPERSTAR

CHRIS KREIE

darbycreek

MINNEAPOLIS

Darby Creek
A division of Lerner Publishing Group, Inc.
241 First Avenue North
Minneapolis, MN 55401 USA

For reading levels and more information, look up this title at www.lernerbooks.com.

The images in this book are used with the permission of: iStockphoto.com/walik; iStockphoto.com/Purdue9394; iStockphoto.com/PhonlamaiPhoto; iStock.com/ sumnersgraphicsinc.

Main body text set in Janson Text LT Std 12/17.5.
Typeface provided by Adobe Systems.

Library of Congress Cataloging-in-Publication Data

Names: Kreie, Chris, author.
Title: The superstar / Chris Kreie.
Description: Minneapolis: Darby Creek, 2018. | Series: Kick! | Summary: Daniela and Rinad's friendship is tested when soccer ace Kennedy joins their high school team.
Identifiers: LCCN 2017016312 (print) | LCCN 2017032203 (ebook) | ISBN 9781541500365 (eb pdf) | ISBN 9781541500242 (lb : alk. paper) | ISBN 9781541500358 (pb : alk. paper)
Subjects: | CYAC: Best friends—Fiction. | Friendship—Fiction. | Soccer—Fiction. | Jealousy—Fiction. | High schools—Fiction. | Schools—Fiction.
Classification: LCC PZ7.K8793 (ebook) | LCC PZ7.K8793 Su 2018 (print) | DDC [Fic]—dc23

LC record available at https://lccn.loc.gov/2017016312

Manufactured in the United States of America
1-43656-33473-8/29/2017

DANIELA gasped for air as she tried to keep the player from Falcon Ridge in front of her. Her name was Kennedy, and Daniela had been chasing after her all game. Daniela didn't always get to know the names of players from other teams, but this girl was different. Kennedy was a special player, maybe the most talented player the Bay Park Rams had ever faced.

Daniela did everything in her power to prevent a goal. She had a million things racing through her mind at once. *Watch Kennedy and the ball. Be ready to move backward or to either side. Don't fall for any fakes. Don't lunge for the ball.* The only teammate behind her was the goalie. If Daniela didn't stop Kennedy, a goal was almost certain. She gritted her teeth and focused.

Suddenly, Kennedy made a move to her left. Daniela moved with her. In an instant, Kennedy shifted her weight and pushed the ball from her left foot to her right. Daniela couldn't keep up. Kennedy shot by to the right and dribbled toward the goal. Daniela scrambled to catch up, but all she could do was watch. Without pausing to line up her shot, Kennedy planted her left foot and struck the ball hard with her right. It curved perfectly in the air around the outstretched hand of the goalie and into the back of the net.

The rest of the Falcon Ridge Flyers raced over to celebrate. It was Kennedy's third goal of the game, and it had tied the score at three to three late in the second half.

Daniela bent over to catch her breath. She was exhausted. She had always considered herself a talented defender and felt like she could play with anyone, but at the moment she wasn't so sure. It would take her best effort to keep Kennedy from scoring again. Maybe more than her best. Plus, Daniela still needed to find a way to help her team score the winning goal.

When play resumed, Daniela and the Rams had possession. The referee glanced at her watch, and Daniela knew they had only a few more minutes to score before the end of regulation time.

The ball was played back to her. She kept it on her foot, trying to lure one of the Flyers toward her. It worked. As the opposing player got close, Daniela kicked the ball across the field to her teammate, Claire. Without pausing to see if her pass connected, Daniela pushed up the field. Claire got to the ball, dribbled it forward, and kept it away from the Flyers along the sideline.

Claire saw an opening and delivered the ball to the middle of the field and the waiting foot of another Rams player. Daniela shouted to get her teammate's attention. "Left!" Daniela was free of Flyers defenders and was racing up the left side. Her teammate spotted her and sent the ball sailing hard in that direction. Daniela stopped. The ball was coming in high. She leaped and knocked it down with her chest. Then she immediately swept it forward with her right foot and continued down the field.

"Daniela!" The shout came from the middle of the field. "Center!" It was Rinad, Daniela's best friend and teammate. Rinad had found an opening in the defense, directly in front of the goal. Daniela took one more step and aimed a pass. A good pass could be the difference between a win and a tie. She kicked the ball with her left foot. It bounced twice on the turf. A player from the Flyers lunged to kick the ball away but missed. Another player tried to use her body to prevent Rinad from getting to the ball, but Rinad was too strong. She shook off the defender and sprinted to meet the ball. The goalie ran out of the net to stop her, but it was too late. Rinad wasted no time and blasted the ball past the diving goalie for the score.

"Yes!" Daniela screamed as she ran to embrace Rinad.

"Awesome pass!" shouted Rinad.

"Awesome goal!" Daniela replied. They hugged as their teammates gathered to celebrate.

Just thirty seconds after play resumed, the referee blew three long blasts with her whistle. The game ended in a Rams victory.

Daniela, Rinad, and their teammates gathered around their coach, then everyone lined up to shake hands with the Flyers. Daniela let her handshake with Kennedy last a few seconds longer than the others. "Great game," Daniela said. "I couldn't stop you."

"Thanks," said Kennedy. "You were tough. You're the best defender I've faced all year."

Daniela smiled. "Really? I appreciate you saying that." Rinad stood silently by Daniela's side, waiting for the line to start moving again.

"You never dove for the ball," said Kennedy. "Not once. I usually wait for the defender to go for the ball and then I make my move. You have amazing patience." She paused. "Hey, maybe we should practice together sometime."

"Really?"

"Yeah. I don't live too far away. We could meet halfway."

Daniela nodded. "I'd like that."

Kennedy looked at Rinad. "You too, if you

want." Rinad didn't say anything, and Kennedy shrugged. "All right then." She turned back to Daniela. "You can find me online. Kennedy Higgins." Then she smiled and moved down the line.

"I'll do that!" Daniela shouted after her.

After the handshakes, the two friends walked toward the bench. Rinad turned to Daniela. "That was weird with Kennedy."

"Was it?"

"You're not really going to practice with her, are you?"

They grabbed their water bottles and towels. "I don't know," said Daniela, sweat dripping from her forehead. She guzzled her water. "Maybe. She seems nice."

Rinad shook her head. "Last I checked, she plays for another team. She's the enemy. She probably just wants to get in your head so she can beat you next time."

"You're so dramatic." Daniela chuckled and pounded down more of her water. Her heartbeat was slowing. "Besides, she beat me *this* time. We won, but I couldn't stop her."

Rinad stared across the field. "Now that's definitely weird," she said.

"What?"

"Over there." Rinad pointed toward the visitor's bench.

Daniela turned her head. Their coach was talking with one of the Flyers. "That's Kennedy with Coach Mendez," said Daniela.

The Flyers' coach was there too. Their body language made it obvious to Daniela that they weren't having a casual, light-hearted chat. The conversation appeared serious.

Rinad shrugged. "Strange."

Strange was right. Daniela had seen Coach Mendez congratulate opponents before. That was nothing new. But to have a long talk with a player from another team and her coach after the handshakes were over? That was different. Daniela wondered what was going on.

DANIELA bounced the soccer ball from knee to knee. She dropped it to her foot and gently kicked it to Rinad, who was standing about six feet away. Rinad flipped the ball into the air and sent it back toward Daniela with her head. It was a few days after their game against the Flyers. The Rams were warming up before practice.

Rinad stepped on the ball when it came to her again. "Did you hear about Falcon Ridge?"

"I heard something about the team forfeiting the rest of the season," said Daniela. "I assumed it was a rumor."

"It's not," said Rinad. "Anyway, that's what I heard. I guess they're having some kind of budget crisis and had to cancel most of their sports programs."

"That can happen?" Daniela used her left foot to kick the ball into the air behind her. Then she spun and kicked it back to Rinad.

"Apparently."

"What a terrible way to end a season," said Daniela. "They were a good team, I feel bad for their players."

"Especially for Kennedy, your new best friend," said Rinad.

Daniela shook her head and gave Rinad half a smile. "She's not my 'new best friend.'"

"You seemed pretty tight the other day."

"She's a nice person," said Daniela. "And yes, I do feel bad for her. She's probably the best soccer player I've ever seen and now she doesn't have a team to play for. I'd be so angry if that happened here."

"We can agree on that," said Rinad.

The sound of a whistle suddenly ended their conversation. "Everyone over here!" Coach Mendez yelled.

As Daniela scooped up the ball and turned toward Coach Mendez, she froze. She had been completely unaware that someone else had arrived on the field during warm-ups. That someone was now standing right next to Coach Mendez.

"Rinad!" Daniela whispered as she caught up to her friend. "Look. It's Kennedy."

Rinad frowned. "What's she doing here?"

"Girls!" Coach Mendez was shouting and waving in their direction.

"Come on," said Rinad. "We have to get over there."

"Ladies," said Coach Mendez. "You probably recognize the player standing next to me since we just played against her former team. This is Kennedy, from Falcon Ridge."

"Hi, everyone." Kennedy gave a little wave.

"I'm not going to give you all the details because truthfully it's none of your business," said Coach Mendez. "But to make a long story short, Kennedy's team had to forfeit the rest of their season."

The Rams players all began talking at once.

Coach Mendez clapped her hands. "Now listen up. In order for Kennedy to keep playing soccer, she decided to transfer schools. And lucky for us, she chose to come to Bay Park. She's a Ram now. I hope you'll go out of your way to make her feel at home. We're lucky to have her."

"Thanks, Coach Mendez," said Kennedy. The Rams gathered around to greet their new teammate.

Daniela waited for her turn to say hello. Kennedy beamed at her. "Oh, hi!"

"Looks like we won't have to meet halfway to practice together," said Daniela with a smile. "We'll get to do that every day now."

"I'm excited," said Kennedy.

"Me too." Daniela gave her a hug.

In reality, though, Daniela had mixed feelings about her new teammate. Adding a proven scorer to the Rams was a no-brainer, and Kennedy seemed like a really cool person. But Daniela worried that Kennedy might have a negative effect on team chemistry. The girls were close—like a family. Most of them had been playing together for years. Bringing in a new star player at this point could mess that up. And it was pretty clear that Rinad already didn't like her.

Daniela thought about the season so far. The Rams had won their first three games, and they seemed to be playing better every week. Would Kennedy fit in? Or would she ruin everything?

AFTER Kennedy was introduced to the team, the Rams began practice as usual. The players partnered up and stood facing each other. One player would throw the ball to her partner, who would try to kick it out of the air and send it back. Daniela and Rinad paired up. Kennedy joined Claire just a few feet away.

Daniela had always been good at this drill, priding herself on kicking the ball back to her partner every time without messing up. As she and Rinad practiced, Daniela watched Kennedy out of the corner of her eye. Kennedy moved with grace and confidence. Rinad often had to stretch or lunge to catch balls from Daniela, but Claire barely had to move. Each time Kennedy kicked the ball, she sent it straight to Claire. Her passes were incredibly precise.

The next drill was similar, but the idea was to head the ball back to your partner. Daniela had a hard time keeping her eyes off Kennedy, who was putting on a show nearby.

Daniela's next pass went wildly over Rinad's head. "Hey!" shouted Rinad, going back to retrieve the ball. "I'm not seven feet tall."

"Sorry," said Daniela. She was distracted by Kennedy. The new girl moved like a dancer, gliding easily to the ball. Every header went back perfectly to her partner.

After a few minutes, Coach Mendez blew her whistle. "One touch!" she shouted. "Line it up! Gold versus blue!"

Daniela loved this drill. It gave her an opportunity to show off her defending skills.

"Gold at the net," shouted Coach Mendez. "Blue at the cone." Daniela and Rinad lined up with the other players wearing gold vests next to the goal. Their teammates dressed in blue lined up behind Claire at an orange cone about fifteen yards from the goal.

"Kennedy, you know this one?" asked the coach.

"I'll catch on," Kennedy responded. She went to the back of line with the other blue players.

Rinad was first. She kicked the ball over to Claire at the cone. Then Rinad raced out to try to stop Claire from scoring. Claire controlled the ball and pushed it forward. Before Rinad could get there, Claire blasted the ball past the arms of the goalie and into the net.

"Nice shot!" shouted Coach Mendez.

Daniela was next. She was fired up and ready to show Kennedy what she could do. After passing the ball to a player at the cone she sprinted forward and easily took the ball away before her opponent had a chance to take a shot. "Perfect defending!" yelled Coach Mendez.

Each player went through the drill a few times. Kennedy scored a goal every time she was up. She made it look easy.

Daniela made a bunch of good defensive stops, never letting the player she faced score a goal. She felt good about how she was doing, but she hadn't gone up against Kennedy yet. Would Kennedy be able to score on Daniela as easily as she had on everyone else?

Finally, Daniela and Kennedy faced off. As she stood near the goal, Daniela could sense the eyes of her teammates watching. She was the Rams' best defender, and Kennedy was the team's new hot shot—something had to give. Daniela wanted to prove that she had the skills to stop her talented new teammate.

She took a deep breath and sent the ball forward. Kennedy controlled the ball and kicked it smoothly a few feet forward and to the right. Daniela sprinted in that direction. Kennedy raised her foot for a shot. Daniela went for the block but quickly realized the shot was a fake. She slowed down and got her body under control, keeping her eye on the ball.

Kennedy's next move happened fast. She rolled her right foot over the ball and sent it to her left foot, then back again to her right. Kennedy attempted one more dribble to the left, but Daniela guessed correctly this time.

She attacked the ball with her right foot and sent it sailing toward the middle of the field. Her teammates cheered.

"Excellent!" yelled Coach Mendez.

"Nice play," said Kennedy, holding out her fist.

"Thanks." Daniela gave her a fist bump.

"I can already tell moving to Bay Park was a good idea," said Kennedy as they stepped out of the way of the next two players. "Going up against you all the time is going to make me a better player."

"I feel the same way." Daniela smiled. "You're going to challenge me. That'll make me better—hopefully." She laughed. Kennedy was tough, but she seemed to be a great teammate. Maybe there was no reason to worry about team chemistry after all. Kennedy had the potential to be the last, perfect piece in the Rams' championship season.

"Water break!" shouted Coach Mendez.

Daniela joined Rinad on the sidelines.

"She's good," said Rinad between sips of water.

"You think?" said Daniela sarcastically.

"She's maybe too good."

"What do you mean?"

"I mean I've worked hard the past two seasons to earn a spot as a starting forward," said Rinad. "Finally, my senior year, I make that happen. Now this new girl shows up and she's going to ruin it for me. She's going to take my spot."

"You don't know that," said Daniela.

"She's better than I am, that's for sure," Rinad said. "It's just a matter of time before she becomes a starter and I go back to the bench."

"Don't be so sure," said Daniela. "Coach Mendez loves you. She's always talking about how hard you work. Even if Kennedy gets a starting spot that doesn't mean you're the one who's going to get benched."

"We'll see," said Rinad.

"*TACO* Tuesday!" Rinad was all smiles as she sat down next to Daniela for lunch the following day in the school cafeteria.

Daniela had already begun to scarf down her soft-shell tacos. "Best day of the week," she said with a grin. Daniela and Rinad didn't have any classes together, so their only real chance to catch up at school was during lunch.

As always, the cafeteria was crowded and loud. Daniela had to raise her voice to be heard over the noise. "How are you feeling about the team?" she asked.

Rinad shrugged between mouthfuls. "Still worried."

"I've been thinking more about the whole Kennedy thing," said Daniela. "I don't think

Coach Mendez is going to put her in the starting lineup."

Rinad rolled her eyes. "Come on. How can you keep someone that good off the field?"

"I think she'll be loyal to you and the other players who have worked so hard these past few years. She's not going to start a new player, just like that." Daniela snapped her fingers. "It wouldn't be fair."

"You've seen Kennedy play," said Rinad. "She's the best scorer on the team. No way Coach Mendez is going to keep her on the bench. Besides, that's why she moved here—to play."

"Hey, speak of the devil," Daniela said. She nodded toward the front of the room. Rinad turned around to see Kennedy walking across the cafeteria toward them, a food tray in her hands.

"Put your head down," said Rinad. She covered her face with her hand.

"Why?" asked Daniela. Kennedy had made eye contact with Daniela and was heading straight for them. "Too late, she's coming this way."

"Hi, girls," she said when she made it to their table.

"Hi," said Daniela. Rinad didn't say anything.

"Can I join you?"

"Of course," said Daniela. Rinad glared at her. Daniela responded with a tiny shrug of her shoulders.

Kennedy sat down. "You guys are lucky. This cafeteria is way better than my old one at Falcon Ridge. Most days our food was impossible to eat. Some days it was impossible even to identify." She laughed. "This stuff looks really good."

"Well, you know, it's hard to go wrong with tacos." Daniela put her head down and ate.

After a minute or two of awkward silence Kennedy spoke up again. "What's with that Mr. Mills?" she asked. "I have him for world history and it's a literal snooze fest. Four or five kids fell asleep and he didn't even try to wake them up."

"I had him last year for civics," said Daniela. "Yeah, he was pretty boring." Rinad was finished eating, but she continued to say nothing.

"Have you ever had a class with him, Rinad?" asked Kennedy.

"Nope."

"You're lucky," said Kennedy.

Daniela went back to her food. The conversation fizzled again, and the three of them sat without talking. Daniela felt bad. Normally she would go out of her way to be nice and welcoming to a new student, especially a teammate. But she didn't want to be too friendly with Kennedy. She knew that Rinad viewed her as the enemy, and Daniela didn't want to turn her back on her best friend.

Kennedy finally broke the silence. "I'm really excited for the rest of the season. You guys have a great team. I just hope I can contribute and make us even better."

Daniela was becoming more and more uncomfortable. Kennedy seemed so nice, and she was clearly trying hard to be friendly. "You will," said Daniela. She stared at Rinad and raised an eyebrow in a silent plea for her to make more of an effort. Rinad just stared back.

Kennedy looked around the cafeteria, then down at her food. She sat that way for several seconds and then glanced up at Daniela. Her smiled had disappeared. She shook her head, grabbed her tray and stood up. "Nice talking to you guys." Daniela could tell she didn't mean it. Kennedy turned and walked away.

"Finally," said Rinad, as she watched Kennedy take a seat at another table. "That was brutal."

"It was rude," said Daniela. "That's what it was."

"Hey," said Rinad. "Now she knows she has to earn our respect."

"Respect is one thing," Daniela said. "But she at least deserved some basic courtesy from us."

"Whatever." Rinad waved her hand dismissively.

Daniela felt awful. She hated the way they had just treated Kennedy. That wasn't the person she wanted to be.

Her thoughts turned to the team. Her fears about negative team chemistry came rushing back. Rinad was making things complicated, and it looked like Daniela was going to have to take sides. Being friends with both Rinad and Kennedy didn't seem possible.

PRACTICE the next two days was a
balancing act. To keep Rinad happy, Daniela
kept her distance from Kennedy in the locker
room and during warm-ups. But she couldn't
avoid her during practice. She and Kennedy
combined several times for outstanding plays.
Daniela couldn't help it that Kennedy was a
lot of fun to play with. She always got open for
Daniela's passes and made countless little plays
to make her teammates better.

The problem was that the better Kennedy
played, the more upset Rinad became.
Daniela continued to stick by her friend's side,
encouraging her as much as she could.

Thursday afternoon, the Rams played a
home game against the Fairfield Titans. It was

their first game with Kennedy on the roster. Daniela was relieved that Coach Mendez included Rinad in the starting lineup. Kennedy would start the game on the bench.

"I told you there was nothing to worry about," Daniela said to Rinad.

"I better do well," said Rinad. "I need to show Coach Mendez I deserve that starting spot."

"Don't be nervous," said Daniela. "Just play your game."

The Rams started strong. They controlled the play early in the first half, keeping the Titans moving backward and on their heels. The Rams had several scoring opportunities, including three corner kicks. On one of the corners, Daniela kicked a beautiful bender to the front of the goal. The ball sailed just over the heads of several Titans defenders and drifted to the far corner. Rinad was right there, in perfect position for an open shot, but she whiffed on it and the ball rolled out of bounds.

"Don't get down on yourself!" Daniela shouted. "You'll get another chance." Rinad nodded as she ran back up the field.

Finally, the Rams made the most of an opportunity. Daniela got into position in the middle of the field as her team controlled the ball. A Rams player took a long shot toward the goal, but a Titans defender headed it away. Daniela was in perfect position. She collected the header with her right foot and then pushed the ball to her left. The player in front of her couldn't keep up. Daniela sped forward and made a perfect pass to Rinad, who quickly kicked the ball over to Claire at the right side of the goal. Claire received the pass and smacked a gorgeous shot into the net.

The Rams rushed together to celebrate. Claire jumped into Daniela's arms as Rinad joined them. "Great shot," said Daniela.

"Awesome pass, Rinad," said Claire.

"Thanks."

Daniela looked to the sidelines. The girls from the bench were on their feet. Kennedy held her arm high in the air and raised a fist toward the players on the field. Daniela pumped her fist in return.

Just before halftime, the Titans managed a goal of their own on a corner kick. The score remained tied well into the second half as both teams tightened up their defense. Neither side had any serious scoring opportunities. After a long shot by the Titans flew wildly over the goal, Daniela looked to the sideline and noticed that Coach Mendez was subbing two players into the game. One of them was Kennedy.

Kennedy sprinted onto the field. "Rinad!" she shouted. Kennedy was taking Rinad's place on the field.

Oh no, thought Daniela. *This won't be good.* Rinad jogged off the field with her head down.

"Let's go, girls!" yelled Kennedy. "Time for a goal!"

Daniela got into position. The Rams' goalie got play started again with a long kick that sailed deep into Titans' territory. A Rams player tracked the ball down and controlled it along the right side of the field. She passed to a teammate who quickly sent it on to Daniela near the left sideline. It was a perfect pass that hit her in stride. She kicked the ball ahead and streaked past the defender in front of her. That's when she spotted Kennedy, who was open to her right. Daniela quickly sent the ball to her new teammate.

From there, Kennedy took over. She nimbly avoided one defender and kept her foot on the ball as another Titans player raced over. Without missing a beat, Kennedy looked up and made eye contact with Daniela. She gave a quick nod, and Daniela immediately understood what she wanted. Daniela broke toward the goal, and Kennedy hit her with a pass. As soon as the ball left her foot, Kennedy dashed around her defender and into the center of the field. It was a classic give-and-go. Daniela received the pass and immediately sent it back to Kennedy, who drilled the ball past the goalie and into the net.

Kennedy lifted her arms and ran over to embrace Daniela. "Excellent pass!" she shouted.

"That was amazing!" Daniela had a huge smile on her face. Then the rest of the team arrived to celebrate.

The players ran back to their spots.

Kennedy clapped her hands. "Let's get another one!" she shouted.

Daniela felt great. She couldn't wipe the smile from her face. The mess between Rinad and Kennedy had temporarily drifted to the back of her mind. Her thoughts were on soccer and the excitement and beauty of a perfect goal. Playing with Kennedy couldn't be more fun.

AFTER Kennedy's goal, the Rams played
with more fire. They maintained the offensive
pressure and allowed the Titans to clear the
ball out of their end just twice the rest of
the game.

With only a few minutes remaining,
Daniela controlled the ball in the corner of
the field. She had a Titans defender on her
and several teammates open near the goal. If
she could beat the defender, she could set up a
teammate for a good shot. She danced over the
ball, passing it between her feet as the defender
tried to keep Daniela in front of her. Daniela
wanted the Titans' player to make the first
move so she could dribble around her and get
into the open.

Daniela's patience paid off. The defender made a play on the ball, and Daniela quickly pushed the ball to the right and scooted around her. She looked to pass, but suddenly another Titans player swooped in and tackled the ball away, kicking it out of bounds. "Corner kick!" shouted the referee.

Kennedy gave Daniela a thumbs-up. "Great play!" she shouted.

Daniela ran to the corner and positioned the ball gently on the grass. She wiped a strand of sweaty hair from her forehand and concentrated on the kick. She had done a million corner kicks in her life. There was nothing to it.

She paused, looked up to see that her teammates were ready, and then stepped toward the ball. She hit it cleanly and followed through, watching the ball curve neatly through the air into the goal area. She noticed that Kennedy was a few steps behind the rest of the players, farther from the goal than the rest of them. As the ball approached, Kennedy made her move. She took two steps and jumped into the air, striking the ball with her head before anyone else could get to it. The goalie never had a chance. The ball rocketed past her and into the goal.

Daniela sprinted onto the field, and Kennedy gave her a high five. "Perfect kick," she said.

"What a goal," said Daniela. "You soared for that thing."

"I love headers," Kennedy said with a smile. "Think we've got a few more of those in us this season?"

"I think so."

Just a few minutes later, the referee blew her whistle. The game was over. The Rams came together to celebrate their win and shake hands with the Titans.

Kennedy gave Daniela a big hug. Then Daniela spotted Rinad sitting by herself on the sideline.

"Ready to head in?" Kennedy asked.

"I'll be there in a minute," said Daniela. She jogged over and took a seat next to Rinad. "What a game, huh?"

"You guys looked good," she said.

"You too," said Daniela. "You played really well."

"Apparently not well enough."

"Coach subs people in and out all the time," said Daniela. "Without you, we never would have scored that first goal."

"Maybe."

"That's a fact," said Daniela.

They sat quietly for a minute while the players continued to clear the field.

"My corner kick was pretty good, don't you think?" Daniela bumped Rinad with her shoulder, hoping to get a smile out of her.

"Sure."

Daniela looked out toward the field, then back at Rinad. "Are you mad at me?" she asked.

"No."

"Are you sure?" asked Daniela.

Rinad turned her eyes to the ground and away from Daniela. One of her legs bounced up and down with nervous energy.

"If you're mad, you can tell me." Daniela was beginning to get frustrated.

Rinad looked at her. "You found a new friend," she said. "I guess you don't need me anymore."

"What are you talking about?" asked Daniela. "Of course I need you."

"You and Kennedy seem pretty tight already," said Rinad. "I saw you guys hugging and celebrating together and stuff."

"We're teammates now," said Daniela. "That's what teammates do."

"Whatever. If you were really my friend you would see that I need you right now and you wouldn't be hanging out with Kennedy."

"We weren't hanging out," said Daniela. "We were just talking."

Rinad got to her feet.

"Don't leave," said Daniela standing up. "Can we talk about this?"

"There's nothing else to say." Rinad turned her back and walked away.

"Rinad!" But Rinad didn't stop. Daniela was left standing by herself. She wanted to chase after her, but she realized it would probably do no good. Rinad was clearly in no mood to talk. Daniela realized her best strategy was to leave her alone and give her the space she needed. Let her cool down and try again tomorrow.

The joy of the victory felt like a distant memory. Daniela walked to the locker room feeling nothing but concern and confusion.

DANIELA thought about Rinad the moment she woke up on Saturday morning. She had so many emotions running through her head. Part of her felt bad for Rinad and understood why she was upset about Kennedy joining the team. But another part of her felt that Rinad was being childish and selfish. Kennedy was a great player—of course Coach Mendez wanted her on the field. And it wasn't fair of Rinad to expect Daniela to snub Kennedy. Kennedy had tried to connect with both of them. She had been nothing but friendly since she arrived at Bay Park. Rinad was being completely unreasonable and immature.

The bottom line, though, was that Daniela loved Rinad. She loved her like a best friend and a sister. It was a love she imagined would be in her life forever. The two of them had been friends since elementary school. They talked about going to the same college to study astronomy and being bridesmaids at each other's weddings. Rinad was the best friend Daniela had ever had. She wasn't about to let this situation with Kennedy come between them.

After breakfast, Daniela texted Rinad a few times with no response. Finally, she gave her a call.

"Hi," said Rinad when she picked up.

"Hi," responded Daniela. She was lying on her bed, staring at the ceiling. "How're you doing?"

"I'm fine." There was a long pause on the other end. Finally she said, "How are you?"

"I'm good. I'm glad you answered." Daniela thought it would be smart to keep the conversation away from soccer. "My mom brought me a donut from the grocery store this morning," she said. "It made me think about you. It was your favorite, a bear claw with chocolate toes."

"Yum," said Rinad. "Jealous." There was another long pause. "I heard there's a new donut shop opening up by the mall. One of those gourmet places where they put weird things like bacon and cereal on the donuts."

"We'll have to go check it out when it opens." Daniela smiled and rolled over.

"Sounds like a plan," said Rinad.

"What else is going on?" asked Daniela. And just like that, things between them seemed normal again, almost as if Kennedy had never entered their lives. The conversation lasted almost an hour. They talked about donuts and homework and shopping, and made plans to watch a meteor shower. They were friends again, just like before.

When Monday rolled around, Daniela felt great. Practice that afternoon was a joy. The sun was shining, a cool breeze was blowing across the field, and Daniela had her best friend back. The team was in high spirits after their impressive win the week before.

"Scrimmage!" yelled Coach Mendez following thirty minutes of drills. "Starters from last week in gold, the rest of you in blue!"

Daniela loved to scrimmage. She jogged over to Rinad, who was putting on her gold vest. "Let's do this," she said, patting her on the back.

"Time to score some goals," said Rinad.

Daniela stayed locked onto Kennedy, who was on the blue team. She did a good job, keeping the ball off Kennedy's foot most of the time and setting up teammates for scoring opportunities. At one point Daniela kicked a ball that arced high and came down in front of the goal. Rinad tapped the ball to the ground with her chest, collected it, and turned and fired a shot in one smooth motion. The goalie barely got a hand on it to knock it away. "Nice try!" Daniela told her. Rinad smiled and gave her a thumbs-up.

A few moments later, Daniela saw Rinad streaking up the left side. She passed her the ball, then Rinad kicked a perfect crossing pass to a teammate breaking for the goal. The teammate took a shot that sailed just wide of the net. "Awesome pass!" yelled Daniela.

"You too!" Rinad replied. Daniela smiled. It was like the drama with Kennedy had completely disappeared.

The two teams played a scoreless scrimmage until Kennedy finally got her chance. Running along the left side of the field, just across the centerline, she kept the ball on her foot, dribbling effortlessly down the field. Daniela was in front of her, but she was backing up and having a hard time trying to match Kennedy's speed. Kennedy moved left, then right, and then exploded toward the goal. Daniela tried tackling the ball away, but Kennedy was too quick. Daniela fell to the turf as Kennedy calmly lined up a shot and drilled the ball into the goal.

She was still on the ground when Kennedy ran over and extended her hand to help Daniela up. "Nice play," Kennedy said. "You almost stopped me."

"Nice goal." Daniela looked over and saw that Rinad was watching them.

"OK, that's it!" yelled Coach Mendez. "Practice is over!"

The players gave their vests to the team manager and collected their gear. Daniela stood by the bench and tilted her head back to drain what was left from her water bottle. When she looked back to the field, she noticed that Coach Mendez was talking with Rinad near one of the goals. After a minute or so, the coach patted her on the back and walked away. Rinad stood like a statue, staring at the ground. It didn't look good.

Daniela ran over to Rinad. "What happened?" she asked. She could see that Rinad was crying. Daniela reached out to put her arm around her friend, but Rinad pulled away.

"I told you," said Rinad. "I told you Kennedy was going to replace me."

"Is that what Coach Mendez said?"

Rinad nodded. "I'm out of the starting lineup."

Daniela felt horrible. It was difficult seeing Rinad this way. She wrapped both arms around her. Rinad resisted the hug at first but then leaned her body into Daniela's. "I hope you know I'm just as upset about this as you are," said Daniela.

"Thanks," said Rinad. "That means a lot."

"I'm here for you. And we'll get through this together." She held onto Rinad for a long time.

Suddenly Kennedy was there. "Is everything all right?"

Rinad stepped back from Daniela's embrace. "No, thanks to you," said Rinad.

"What happened?"

"Rinad's a bit shaken up, that's all," said Daniela.

"Why?" asked Kennedy, touching Rinad on the shoulder. "Can I help?"

Rinad flinched. "You took my spot!" she said. The look in Rinad's eyes had quickly turned from sadness to anger. "Don't act like you don't know what's wrong."

"I didn't realize . . ." said Kennedy.

"Rinad," said Daniela. "It's not Kennedy's fault."

"Of course it's Kennedy's fault," Rinad

snapped. "If it wasn't for her I'd still be in the starting lineup."

"I didn't mean to . . ." Kennedy stalled. She obviously didn't know what to say. She looked confused and hurt.

"I hope you're happy," Rinad continued. "The superstar soccer player moves to Bay Park and everyone loves her. Well, now you're in the starting lineup, and you don't care who you had to step on to get there."

"Rinad," said Daniela again. "You know that's not what happened here."

Rinad glared at her. "Whose side are you on anyway? You just said you were going to be there for me."

"I am," said Daniela. "But there's no reason why we can't all be friends. Kennedy didn't hurt you on purpose."

"I see," said Rinad. "I get what's going on here. You're happy about this. Now you get to play with Kennedy and the two of you can be some kind of dynamic duo. It's obvious how much fun you have playing with her. That's what you really wanted from the beginning, isn't it?"

"That's not fair," said Daniela.

"Forget it," said Rinad. "I'm over it." She wiped the tears from her eyes and began to walk away.

Daniela reached out and grabbed her arm, but Rinad jerked it away. "Let go of me!" she shouted. "Please. Just . . . don't."

"I'm sorry, Rinad," said Daniela. She didn't know what else to say.

"Whatever." Rinad pulled her backpack onto her shoulders and walked off.

Daniela sighed as she watched Rinad leave the field. Kennedy looked over at her. "You OK?" she asked.

Daniela shrugged. "We'll see."

ON Tuesday morning, as Daniela headed toward the entrance of the high school, she heard a familiar voice behind her. "Hey, Daniela!" She turned to see Kennedy running over to her. Daniela waited for her to catch up. "How's it going?" Kennedy eased alongside her with a smile.

"Hi," said Daniela. She couldn't help but return the smile. Everything about Kennedy was positive, and it was contagious. "I'm fine. How are you?"

"Doing good," said Kennedy. They strolled up the steps to the school.

"I've been thinking about Rinad," said Kennedy. "I feel bad about what happened."

"It's not your fault. Really, it isn't."

"I know." Kennedy shrugged her shoulders and sighed. "I just wish she wasn't so angry with me."

"She'll be fine eventually," said Daniela. She looked at Kennedy and smiled again. "Can we talk about something else?"

"Of course," said Kennedy. They got to the door, and Kennedy held it open for Daniela. "Ready for the game tonight?"

"Yeah, I'm excited. I'm hoping we can keep our streak alive."

Inside, the hallways were buzzing with students heading to first period classes. Teachers stood in the doorways of their classrooms greeting students.

"I'm really starting to like this place." Kennedy looked at Daniela and smiled.

"I'm glad," said Daniela.

At lunch, Daniela took a spot at her usual table and waited for Rinad. She hadn't spoken with her since practice the day before and was hoping the two of them would have a chance to talk things out. But instead of Rinad, Kennedy showed up.

"Can I join you?" she asked, standing next to Daniela's table.

"Um." Daniela looked around, thinking Rinad might arrive at any minute. "Well." She didn't know what to say. She wanted to eat with Kennedy, but she knew Rinad wouldn't feel the same way. If Rinad saw her sitting with Kennedy, she would never join them, and the most important thing on Daniela's mind was patching things up with her old friend. That wouldn't happen if Kennedy was there. "It's just . . ."

Kennedy looked confused. "Daniela. What is it?"

"I want to eat with you," said Daniela. "I do. But . . ."

"OK then." Kennedy chuckled and started to sit.

"No, you can't!" Daniela snapped. Kennedy flinched in surprise. She took a step back. "I'm sorry," Kennedy stammered. "It's just . . . I don't think it's a good idea for us to eat together today. I'm sorry."

Kennedy looked at her sideways. "OK," she

said. "You know, Daniela, I can't figure you out. Sometimes you're really nice to me. Other times, you act like you want nothing to do with me. You don't make any sense." She turned and walked away. A moment later, Daniela saw her take a seat on the other side of the cafeteria with some other members of the team. They instantly made room for her and looked happy to have her join them.

Daniela buried her head in her hands. *This is such a mess.*

She was in the middle of losing her best friend, and she was completely blowing the opportunity to make a new one. She continued eating her lunch and watching for Rinad, who never showed up.

AFTER school that day, the Rams went on the road to face the Southwest Cyclones. Rinad was already sitting next to another teammate when Daniela boarded the bus. Kennedy had an open spot next to her, but Daniela knew that sitting with Kennedy would only make things worse with Rinad. Daniela sat by herself at the front of the bus for the long ride to Southwest High.

Warm-ups were just as lonely. Rinad didn't talk to Daniela or look at her or come anywhere near her. She was making it pretty clear that she wanted nothing to do with her.

During the game, Daniela tried hard to forget about all the drama with Rinad and Kennedy and just concentrate on soccer. It helped that Kennedy was with her on the field from the beginning. They fed off each other. Daniela was a steady rock on defense and Kennedy was a game-changer up front.

Just minutes into the game, the Cyclones were putting on the pressure, controlling the ball in the Rams' end. *Time to push back*, Daniela thought. Suddenly, three forwards from Southwest went on the attack. One of them dribbled toward the goal on the right side while the other two pushed forward on the left. Daniela knew that if her team could get the ball while the three Southwest players were so deep, the Rams would have a perfect chance for a counterattack.

Seconds later, that's exactly what happened. One of Daniela's teammates made a perfect break on a pass and sneaked between two Cyclones. She intercepted the ball and immediately swept it wide to Daniela.

"Up!" yelled Kennedy. She was near the center circle with a lone Cyclone defender alongside her. Daniela didn't waste any time. She cleared herself from the crowd around her and then hammered the ball up the field. Kennedy waited just long enough to avoid the offside call and then took off. It was a perfect pass, catching Kennedy in stride. She met the ball and turned on the afterburners. Kennedy sped down the field ahead of her defender, made a quick move to confuse the goalie, and shot the ball into the back of the net.

As the Rams celebrated, Kennedy pulled Daniela into a hug. "You have incredible vision," Kennedy said.

"I just put the ball where I knew you could get it," said Daniela. "You did the rest."

In the second half, with the Rams leading the Cyclones 1–0, Kennedy repaid the favor to Daniela. With incredible grace and composure, Kennedy dribbled the ball to the front of the goal, luring three Cyclones defenders to her. Daniela trailed just behind the play. No one was around her. "Open!" she yelled. With a fluid motion that caught the Cyclones by surprise, Kennedy dropped the ball back to Daniela, who sidestepped a Cyclones player dashing awkwardly toward her. With plenty of time to line up her shot, she kicked the ball under the goalie's outstretched arms and into the net.

Another goal a few minutes later put the Rams ahead by three. With the game well in hand, Coach Mendez subbed in the reserves. That included Rinad. She jogged onto the field as Daniela and Kennedy ran off.

"You can do it, Rinad," said Daniela. "Keep up the attack."

Rinad ran past her without saying a word or even making eye contact. Daniela looked at Kennedy, who shrugged.

Daniela went to the far end of the bench to grab her water bottle and towel. She gulped some water and then made her way back to where Kennedy was sitting. "Mind if I join you?" she asked.

"Of course not," said Kennedy. "Great job out there, by the way."

"You too."

"Let's go, girls!" shouted Kennedy, as the Rams fought off a furious Cyclones charge. "Attack the ball!"

They watched the game together, cheering on their teammates. After a few minutes, Daniela got the courage to speak up. "Hey, Kennedy?"

"Yeah?"

"I'm really sorry about today. About lunch. I was really rude to you."

"Don't worry about it." Kennedy put her head down and began kicking at the dirt in front of the bench. "Is there something about me you don't like?"

The question hit Daniela hard. It made her feel awful. She had always thought of herself as a friendly person. The kind of person who reaches out to other people and tries to make them feel better. Never in a million years would she want a teammate—especially an awesome teammate like Kennedy—to think she didn't like her.

"No, it's not that," she said. "It's not that at all. I think you're great. And I love playing soccer with you."

"I feel the same way," said Kennedy. "But I can tell you don't feel comfortable around me. I assume it's because of Rinad?"

Daniela hesitated. She wanted to open up to Kennedy, but she was afraid she'd say something that would make things even more difficult between them. "It's been really hard since you came here," Daniela said. "You're this superstar player, and right away she started to worry she would lose playing time to you. And she was obviously right to worry."

"I know she's your friend," said Kennedy.

"She's my *best* friend," said Daniela. "You took her spot, which has been really hard for her. She's upset and she's taking out her anger on you. And on top of that she thinks I'm betraying our friendship whenever I talk to you or act nice to you. I know it must sound ridiculous and dramatic and all that, but . . ."

"I get it." Kennedy smiled. "If I lost my starting spot to a new girl I'd be pretty ticked off too."

"I don't know what to do," said Daniela. "I'd really like to hang out with you, but Rinad means the world to me. She's been my best friend for as long as I can remember."

Just then the referee blew her whistle, ending the game. Daniela and Kennedy stood up. "You take care of things with Rinad," said Kennedy. "That's important."

"Thanks," said Daniela. "I appreciate that." They began walking toward the middle of the field. "I meant what I said, though. I really do hope we can be friends."

"Me too." Kennedy playfully punched her in the arm. "But first we need to celebrate!" She ran away from Daniela to join the team.

Daniela smiled and ran to catch up.

DANIELA didn't expect Rinad to sit with her at lunch the following day, but she went to their usual table just in case. She sat for a few minutes eating, waiting, and hoping. After five minutes, she decided that if Rinad hadn't arrived yet she probably never would. She got up and moved to Kennedy's table.

Daniela became more and more frustrated as the day went on. Was Rinad planning to avoid her for the rest of their lives? They couldn't go on like this forever. They had to get past the drama. Daniela decided to confront Rinad before practice and try to get her to talk.

When Daniela entered the locker room after school, most of the players were already there, talking and getting into their practice clothes. She spotted Rinad in the corner, chatting with Claire and another teammate, Jada.

It's now or never, Daniela thought. *No reason to put it off any longer.* She walked over to Rinad. "Hey, girls," she said to the group.

"Hi, Daniela," said Claire.

"Hey," said Jada.

As usual, Rinad ignored her. "Hey, let's go," she said to Claire and Jada. "Let's get outside and kick the ball around before practice starts." She stood up and headed for the exit. "Come on."

"See you out there, Daniela," said Claire. She and Jada followed Rinad out the locker room door.

Daniela was suddenly alone, but she wasn't ready to give in. If patching things up with Rinad meant having to work for it, she was up for the challenge. She changed quickly and went out to the field. She found Rinad playing with Claire, Jada, and a few other girls. They were on one half of the field, trying to score on

Jada, who was in goal. Each player was teamed up with another player, passing back and forth and then shooting. "Can I join you guys?" asked Daniela.

"Of course," said Claire. "Come on in."

"She can't play!" blurted Rinad. She received a pass from Claire and then took a shot that Jada caught. "She doesn't have a partner."

Jada held onto the ball, stopping the game. "I can get one," said Daniela.

"Yeah, grab a partner!" shouted Jada.

"No," said Rinad. "Let's just keep going. We already have enough people. She can start her own game on the other end. Let's go. Jada, toss it out!"

"Wait a minute," said Claire. "That's ridiculous. We have plenty of room. Daniela, find another girl and get in here."

"Jada!" shouted Rinad. "Would you throw the ball in already? Enough talking. Let's play."

"Come on, Rinad," said Claire. "Seriously. What's your problem?"

By this time Daniela had lost her patience.

"Forget it," she said. "If Rinad doesn't want me to play, she can have it her way. I won't play." She began walking away. She was frustrated and angry. Rinad was acting like a child.

Daniela jogged away toward the other end of the field. In her mind she replayed the events of the past few days. She didn't deserve to be treated the way Rinad was treating her. All she had done was be friendly to Kennedy, a girl who was new to school and looking for friends. There was nothing wrong with that, and Daniela had no control over who Coach Mendez put in the starting lineup. Daniela wanted to support Rinad, and she didn't want to lose her as a friend, but at that moment the only emotion she felt toward her was anger.

She spotted Kennedy in the corner of the field, kicking a ball around with a couple of other girls. *Kennedy wants to be my friend, and clearly Rinad doesn't*, she thought to herself. *Why fight it?* "Hey, Kennedy!" she shouted. "Got room for one more?"

"Yeah, get over here!" Kennedy waved to her.

Daniela didn't think twice. She ran over to join the group.

THE Rams had a game the next day. This time they were at home against the Mill Valley Scouts. As Daniela took the field, she glanced up at the sky. The weather matched her mood: cold and gray. She tried to get energized and focused during pregame warm-ups, but all she could think about was Rinad and their friendship, which seemed to be falling apart in front of her eyes. It didn't help that Kennedy was in the starting lineup again and Rinad began the game on the bench.

The Scouts came out hard in the first few minutes of the game. As Daniela made a play on the ball, someone plowed into her from behind and knocked her to the ground. She was quickly reminded of the game they played against Mill Valley the year before—it had gotten very physical. The Scouts were not a fast team, but they were big and tough. They used their shoulders and elbows to clear space and get open for shots. Last year, two players from Mill Valley had gotten ejected from the game for dangerous and aggressive tackles.

Daniela picked herself up and rejoined the action. She sprinted up the field as one of her teammates passed the ball forward to Kennedy. Kennedy made a move on her defender, and then set up Claire with a nice pass for a run toward the goal. Claire charged in and was taken to the ground by a hard tackle from a Mill Valley player. The referee ran over. Daniela expected her to issue a yellow card, but instead the ref just gave them a warning. "Careful, girls," she said. "Let's keep it clean." She blew her whistle and play continued.

The game went back and forth with neither team putting a shot into the goal. At halftime the match was still scoreless.

Several minutes into the second half, Kennedy had the ball along the left side.

Daniela swerved around her defender to get open. Kennedy faked a pass to Daniela, then dribbled right to the front of the goal. A Scouts defender came flying in to tackle the ball away and send it over the end line. The ref blew her whistle and signaled for the Rams' first corner kick of the game.

"Claire, take it!" The command came from Coach Mendez. Most of the time Daniela took corners for the team, but sometimes they switched it up and the job went to Claire. Daniela didn't mind—it meant she would get a chance to put Clair's kick into the back of the net. She was hungry for a goal.

The Rams set up in front of Mill Valley's goal. Daniela hung back a little, hoping no one from the Scouts would notice her. Claire was ready. She placed the ball on the grass, took a few steps back, and stepped forward for the kick. The ball sailed toward the goal. Daniela attacked. She surged forward, keeping her eyes on the ball, hoping to get the timing just right. When it felt like the perfect moment, she pushed off the ground and into the air.

Her timing wasn't as perfect as she'd hoped. Instead of smacking the ball with her head, she crashed into a player from Mill Valley. They went down in a heap. The ball snuck through everyone and bounced out of bounds. Daniela felt a throbbing pain in her face. She had smashed her nose against the Mill Valley player's head.

Daniela got to her knees and touched her nose. She looked at her hand—it was covered in blood.

Suddenly, someone was there to help her. "Out of the way! Everyone, give her some space." Daniela looked up. It was Rinad. She had run in from the bench when Daniela went to the ground. Rinad handed her a towel. "Don't try to get up."

"Thanks," said Daniela. She put the towel to her nose and sat back on the grass.

Kennedy stood nearby with Coach Mendez and the rest of the team. "She should go to the bench and get some ice," Kennedy said.

"She's fine where she is," said Rinad.

"No, seriously," said Kennedy. "When your

nose is bleeding you should put some ice on it. Ice will stop it faster than a towel."

"Just butt out!" snapped Rinad. "Please! We've got it."

"Rinad, it's OK," said Daniela.

"I know my friend," Rinad continued. "And I know she freaks out at the sight of blood. If she gets up too soon she'll puke or pass out."

"She's probably right," said Daniela through the towel. "I don't do well with blood."

"But . . ." Kennedy began.

"Leave us alone," interrupted Rinad. She glared at Kennedy. "For once, would you just leave us alone?"

"I'm just trying to help!" Kennedy burst out. "I know you're convinced that I'm here specifically to ruin your life, but all I want is to be a good teammate!" Daniela saw tears of frustration gathering in Kennedy's eyes.

Rinad looked at Kennedy in stunned silence. It was as if she were really seeing her rival for the first time.

"Everybody calm down," said Coach Mendez, patting Rinad on the back. "You going to be all right?" she asked Daniela.

"Rinad's got me," she said. "We're cool."

After a minute, Daniela felt steady enough to stand. "I'll help you off the field," said Rinad. The players and fans clapped when Daniela stood up.

"Rinad, once you get her to the bench come back out," said Coach Mendez as they walked toward the sideline. "I need you on the field."

"OK!"

Rinad helped Daniela to a seat and grabbed an ice pack. "Hold this to your nose for at least ten minutes."

"OK, doc," said Daniela laughing. "Get out there. You've got a game to win."

Rinad smiled and ran onto the field.

DANIELA watched the rest of the game
from the bench. The rough play continued,
with the Scouts taking several Rams to the
ground on dirty plays. The referee had to work
hard to make sure the tackles were legal and to
keep the game under control.

It was late in the second half when the
Rams finally scored. It began with Kennedy.
As she dribbled up the field and drew two
Scout defenders to her, Rinad kept pace with
her to her right. Kennedy sidestepped the
defenders and kicked a pass to Rinad, who had
found an opening in front of the goal. Rinad
took the pass, tapped the ball ahead, and then
kicked it between the legs of the goalie and
into the net.

The Rams went wild. Everyone mobbed Rinad.

Daniela cheered from the bench. "Great job, Rinad!" She gave high fives to her teammates on the sideline. "Awesome pass, Kennedy!" She couldn't be happier that Rinad was back on the field and contributing to the team. But what she saw next really made her heart soar. Rinad and Kennedy shared a hug. Daniela could hardly believe it. "It's about time," she said.

Daniela watched the rest of the game with tissues stuffed up her nose and a smile on her face. It occurred to her that a vicious blow to the face had led to the happiness she was feeling, and she laughed out loud. Rinad's goal held up as the game winner.

After the game and the handshakes, Daniela was anxious to talk with Rinad. She felt like the moment had finally arrived to patch things up for good, but it would have to wait. Daniela was surrounded by concerned teammates.

"How's your nose?" asked Claire.

"Better already," said Daniela. "I'll be fine."

"It's red," said Jada, reaching out as if she might touch it and then pulling her hand back at the last moment. "And swollen. Is it sore?"

"Yeah, but it's OK," said Daniela. "Really."

"That was a cheap shot," said Claire. "I saw the whole thing. The girl from Mill Valley wasn't even going for the ball."

Daniela craned her neck to find Rinad. "I wouldn't know," she said. "I didn't even see her coming."

"But we did it!" said Claire. She popped Daniela lightly in the shoulder with her fist. "We got fired up after they took you down."

"Yeah, you guys were great," said Daniela, still distracted as she looked for Rinad.

"Team!" shouted Coach Mendez. "Bring it in!"

As the players gathered around their coach, Daniela still didn't see Rinad anywhere. *Where could she be?*

"Great game," said Coach Mendez. "You guys kept your heads and you played clean when it would have been easy to stoop to their level and start taking cheap shots. We didn't play rough. We just played good, aggressive soccer. And our play earned us a hard-fought victory. So be glad we won, and be glad you played the game the right way."

The girls cheered.

"Because of this win and the way you got it," continued Coach Mendez, "I'm rewarding you all with a day off." More cheering. "No practice tomorrow. Enjoy this win, get some rest, and have a relaxing weekend. We have another game Monday—come back ready for it. That's it."

The girls gathered their equipment and walked toward the locker room. Daniela scanned the field. Rinad was still nowhere to be found. For some reason she had disappeared as soon as the game ended.

DANIELA was hoping she would have a chance to talk to Rinad at school on Friday. She texted her a couple of times asking to meet up, but she got no response. Then at lunch she scanned every table in the cafeteria, but there was no sign of her. Daniela was confused. After Rinad had helped her with her bloody nose during the game against the Scouts, she'd assumed the two of them were on their way to putting their friendship back together. She couldn't figure out why Rinad was still avoiding her.

After school, Daniela was home alone in her bedroom. She texted Rinad again, but still got nothing in response. Daniela lay on her bed, staring at the ceiling. It was covered with dozens of stickers Rinad had given her on her fifteenth birthday. They were glow-in-the-dark stars and planets. Daniela and Rinad loved astronomy and the constellations. When Rinad had given the stickers to her, Daniela thought nothing would ever come between them. Their friendship had seemed as eternal as the stars at night.

She sat up. "This is ridiculous." She stormed out of her bedroom and ran down the stairs. She slipped on a pair of shoes, grabbed her jacket, and marched out the front door.

Ten minutes later, Daniela was standing at Rinad's front door, ringing the bell. Rinad's mom answered. "Hi, Daniela. You're here to see Rinad? She's upstairs." Rinad's mom held the door open, and Daniela walked in. "She'll be happy to see you."

"Thanks," said Daniela, taking off her shoes. "I hope so."

Upstairs, Daniela found Rinad's bedroom door closed. She tapped on it lightly, then cracked it open and poked her head in.

Rinad was sitting on her bed, reading. "Can I come in?" asked Daniela.

"Sure," said Rinad. She set her book down.

Daniela stepped inside, and Rinad scooted over on the bed. "You want to sit?"

"OK." Daniela joined her.

"Good game yesterday," said Rinad.

"You had an awesome goal," said Daniela.

"Yeah, it was a good one. It was a great pass from Kennedy."

"It sure was," said Daniela. *OK, enough small talk*, Daniela thought. It was time to say what was really on her mind. "So what's going on?" she asked. "You disappeared after the game, I didn't see you all day, and you haven't answered my texts. Are you still mad at me?"

Rinad looked down at her comforter. "I'm sorry," she said. "I feel horrible. I've been acting like such an infant."

"It's OK."

"No, really," said Rinad. "I've been a real jerk."

"No you haven't," said Daniela.

Rinad turned. She looked directly into Daniela's eyes and raised her eyebrows.

"OK," said Daniela. "Maybe you've been a little bit of a jerk."

She didn't feel the need to bash Rinad further—she was doing a good enough job of that herself.

"I've been avoiding you because I'm so ashamed," continued Rinad. "After the way I've been treating you these past couple of weeks, I just couldn't talk to you. I didn't know what to say."

"I'm your best friend," said Daniela. "We can talk about anything."

Rinad looked at her doubtfully. "You still think of me as your best friend?"

"Of course. Always."

Rinad reached over and gave her a tight hug. "Thanks," said Rinad.

Daniela couldn't see Rinad's face, but she could tell she was crying.

Finally, Rinad pulled back. She wiped her eyes. "It's just . . . I got so angry when I lost my spot to Kennedy. And then when I saw the two of you getting along, I thought I was losing my best friend too. I know it sounds stupid."

"It doesn't sound stupid at all," said Daniela.

Rinad sniffed. "Kennedy's pretty cool, isn't she?"

Daniela nodded. "She's pretty cool." She took a tissue from the box on Rinad's nightstand and handed it to her.

"She's been trying to be nice to me," said Rinad. "And all I've done is blame her for all my problems."

"I think she gets it. She's pretty understanding. She realizes why you'd be upset for losing your starting spot."

"That doesn't excuse the way I've been acting," said Rinad. She blew her nose, a loud honk that echoed through her bedroom. "I definitely owe her an apology too. Do you think the three of us could be friends?"

Daniela smiled. "Of course. I think Kennedy would really like that, actually. And I know I would."

Finally, it seemed she wouldn't have to choose between Kennedy and Rinad after all. *What a relief*, she thought.

"And listen," she added. "No one's ever going to come between us. Not a teammate or anyone else. Our friendship is too strong for that."

They hugged again. Daniela held onto Rinad, a big smile covering her face. Their friendship was finally back to normal. And she had a feeling that her team was about to make the leap from good to unstoppable.

ON Monday the Rams faced the Summit Academy Red Hawks. Daniela and Rinad stretched out together before the game. "I hope you get to play today," said Daniela.

"If not, I'll be the team's loudest cheerleader."

Kennedy jogged by. "Hey, Kennedy!" Rinad stood up and walked over to her. "Good luck out there." Rinad stuck her fist out.

"Thanks." Kennedy returned the fist bump. "You too."

"I'm sorry about the way I've treated you," Rinad said. "Are we cool?"

Kennedy smiled. "Yeah, we're cool."

"Good. Then you and Daniela go out and win this thing."

"We'll do our best," said Kennedy.

Play started with the Red Hawks taking control. It was a tough game for the Rams. Summit had a potent lineup of forwards including April Jennings, a scoring star who had been one of the best players in the state the year before. In order to keep up, the Rams would have to play their best game of the year.

Daniela watched April and did her best to stay close to her whenever the ball was near the Rams' goal. It wasn't easy. Twice April beat Daniela for scoring chances. Luckily, neither play resulted in a goal.

Finally, though, April made her mark. After a player from the Red Hawks made a long run up the left side of the field, April called for the pass. Daniela was a step late, and that was all the room April needed. She struck a bender that curved around the Rams' goalie and into the net. The Red Hawks had the lead.

"We'll get it back," said Kennedy, coming over to pat Daniela on the back. "No worries."

Play resumed, but the Rams couldn't even the score. Instead, April struck again, this time running around two Rams defenders and blasting a long shot into the net. Just like that the score was 2–0. The Rams' winning streak was at risk of coming to an end.

"These ladies are tough," said Daniela as her team huddled together after the goal. "We have to take more chances. I know it could be dangerous to push too far forward. We could leave ourselves open for a counterattack, but I think it's the only way we're going to score."

"She's right," said Kennedy. "We have to take more risks. We have to stop playing it safe."

"OK, then," said Daniela. "Let's go!"

The Rams had the ball following the kickoff. They passed it between one another, keeping possession and waiting for a chance to strike. Claire controlled the ball, looked for an opening, and then made a pass back to Daniela. She held it on her foot, advancing a few steps forward while keeping it away from the Red Hawks player in front of her. Daniela looked across the field. No one was in the clear. Even Kennedy was struggling to get open. Suddenly, Claire broke toward the center. Daniela turned quickly and kicked the ball into the air toward her.

The ball reached Claire at the same time a player from Summit Academy did. They collided violently. Both players cried out in pain and fell to the turf, their bodies tangled. The ball rolled away and the referee blew the whistle.

Everyone ran over to check on them. They had separated themselves from each other, but they both still lay on their backs. "Claire, you OK?" asked Daniela.

"No," said Claire. "It's my ankle."

"Did you hit your head?" asked Coach Mendez. "Should we be worried about a concussion?"

"No," said Claire. "I just landed hard and twisted my ankle."

Coach Mendez examined her. "It doesn't seem to be broken. It's probably a sprain."

Daniela and Kennedy helped her up. Claire tried putting some weight on her right leg, but she called out in pain. "Ahh!"

"Put your arms around your teammates," said Coach Mendez. "Let's get you to the bench and put some ice on it." Claire grabbed onto Kennedy and Daniela as the two of them helped her off the field.

"Your ankle's going to be fine, but you should stay off it for a while," Coach Mendez told Claire on the sideline. "As for this game, you're done." She looked toward the bench. "Rinad!" she barked. "You're in!"

Rinad ran over and put her hand on Claire's shoulder. "We're going to win the game," she said. "We're going to win it for you."

"You better," said Claire.

Daniela, Rinad, and Kennedy jogged onto the field together. "You ready to take control?" asked Rinad. "I'm tired of sitting, I'm ready for some action."

"You know it," said Kennedy.

"I'm ready," said Daniela. Even though she felt bad for Claire, she couldn't help being excited that the three of them were going to be on the field together during a game for the first time.

"Then let's do it!" shouted Rinad. Daniela smiled as they ran to take on the Red Hawks.

FOR the rest of the game, the Rams played with a new spark. It was as if Claire's injury had woken them up.

Just minutes after Rinad entered the game, Daniela controlled the ball. She dribbled near the middle of the field, her defender backing off. Daniela kept her head up, watching Rinad and Kennedy and the rest of her teammates move in front of her. She looked for a player to get open. She waited, and still her defender gave her space. Daniela kept moving forward slowly, inching her way closer and closer to the goal. She knew the Red Hawks' defense would soon close in on her and stop her from getting any nearer to their goal. They wouldn't let her just stroll in for a shot.

Just then, the defender closest to her made a move. She lunged at Daniela, trying to tackle the ball away from her. Daniela changed direction quickly and then danced gracefully around the Red Hawks' player. That's when she saw the opening she'd been waiting for all game. She spotted Rinad moving across the field from the right side. Rinad was open, and Daniela had a clear passing lane.

She wasted no time. She kicked the ball smoothly, arcing it through the air. It bounced once and rolled to Rinad's right foot. She trapped the ball then waited just long enough for two Red Hawks players to sprint toward her. Her timing was perfect. She had drawn attention away from Kennedy, who was open on the left side. Rinad fired a perfect pass. The goalie was completely out of position, and Kennedy one-timed a hard shot into the net.

Daniela and Rinad rushed over to celebrate with Kennedy. They hugged. Moments later the rest of the team joined them. "That's how you do it!" said Daniela.

"Amazing pass!" shouted Kennedy.

"That was awesome," said Rinad. "But we're not done yet."

"Let's go!" Daniela screamed into the air.

Play resumed with the Rams flying all around the field. The Red Hawks looked sluggish. But a minute later the referee blew her whistle, signaling that the first half was over.

On the sideline the Rams felt optimistic. "We can get two more," said Rinad. "Not a problem. I'm good for at least one. Who else?"

Daniela laughed.

"Let's just keep playing hard, ladies," she said. "And smart too. We can definitely beat them if we stay focused."

The second half started with a bang. Rinad took a pass from Kennedy in the far left corner. After clearing herself from her defender, Rinad lofted a floating pass across the field and into the box in front of the goal. Daniela was on the spot. She kept a defender away with her shoulder and got her foot on the ball at just the right moment. Without pausing, she sent a booming shot toward the goal. The goalie stood ready with her arms out, but she didn't have time to react. She stood flat-footed as the ball blew past her into the net. The game was suddenly tied at two.

Things tightened up after that. Both teams played with caution, worried that taking a chance could give their opponent an opportunity to score in the other direction. The minutes ticked by. Neither team had a serious scoring chance.

A Red Hawks player tackled the ball away from Daniela along the left sideline, and it rolled out of bounds. Before she could throw the ball back in, Kennedy ran over to her. "I just talked to Rinad," she said. "She'll get open so you can pass to her. And I'll be a decoy. Keep your eyes on me. That should draw a couple players in my direction, which just might give Rinad the space she needs."

"OK," said Daniela. "Good plan." She was impressed that Kennedy and Rinad were already so in sync.

Kennedy grinned at her. "Let's make it happen!" She jogged into position.

Daniela collected the ball and got ready for the throw-in. Kennedy stood in the middle of the field with a defender glued to her. Daniela kept her gaze locked on her while still trying to see Rinad and the rest of the action out of the corner of her eye.

Kennedy broke backward, drawing her defender with her. Daniela lifted the ball over her head. Kennedy shouted, "I'm open!" She was doing a terrific job acting like the ball was coming to her. Another Red Hawks player moved toward her.

Suddenly, Daniela looked away from Kennedy. She and Rinad made eye contact, and Rinad made her break. Daniela cocked the ball behind her head and flung it as hard as she could, trying her best to catch Rinad in stride.

The rest was all Rinad. She knocked the ball down in a full sprint and never stopped. Her speed caught every Red Hawks defender by surprise. She glided around one defender to the right. She sprinted past another one on the left. It was like the ball was attached to her foot by a string. Daniela jogged forward, but mostly she just watched.

Two more defenders ran toward Rinad. She changed direction and raced around them to the right. There was just one Red Hawks player between her and the goalie. The defender stepped to her right to slow Rinad down, but her effort was wasted. Rinad blew past her, and without pausing to aim, she kicked a gorgeous shot high toward the top left corner of the goal. The goalie stretched, but she couldn't get more than the tips of her fingers on the ball. The Rams had taken the lead!

Daniela and Kennedy and their teammates ran toward Rinad. Rinad sprinted to the corner of the field as everyone chased after her. She dropped to her knees and slid several feet along the grass, her arms held high and her face toward the sky. A second later, her teammates caught up and dove on top of her. They cheered, laughed, and hugged. Rinad had just scored the most incredible goal Daniela, or any of the rest of them, had ever seen.

"That was amazing!" Daniela had her hands on Rinad's shoulders and was shaking her.

Rinad smiled. "It was, wasn't it? I wasn't sure I had it in me."

"I never doubted it," said Kennedy.

"Me either," said Daniela.

The game ended moments later.

"Bring it in!" Coach Mendez yelled from the sideline. The Rams jogged over. Daniela, Kennedy, and Rinad locked arms as they listened to their coach.

"You guys made me very proud out there," said Coach Mendez. "You didn't give up when you were down by two goals up against a very talented team. You deserve this one!"

The girls cheered.

"I don't normally like to single out individual players," said Coach Mendez. "But today I'm going to do that."

"All right, Rinad!" shouted Kennedy. Everyone laughed.

"That's right," said Coach Mendez. "I want to especially congratulate Rinad, but not for the reason you're probably thinking. She scored a huge goal for us, a goal that was one of the most spectacular I've ever seen as a coach, by the way."

Daniela squeezed Rinad's arm. They shared a smile.

"I want to congratulate her for another reason," said Coach Mendez. "Rinad, as you know, began the season in the starting lineup but was replaced by Kennedy. That couldn't have been easy. But Rinad kept practicing hard and waiting for her moment. Well, let me tell you. That moment came today!"

"That's right!" shouted Daniela. The team laughed and cheered.

"Rinad made the most of her opportunity," said Coach Mendez. "This team became a lot stronger today, and we have a lot to be excited about for the future. Let's soak up this victory and come back for another one on Thursday. Congratulations, girls!"

The team let out a loud, long cheer. Daniela, Rinad, and Kennedy kept their arms linked and formed a circle. "Nothing's better than a win," said Kennedy.

"Nothing's better than doing it with your friends," said Daniela.

"All of them," said Rinad.

Daniela looked at Kennedy and then at Rinad.

"It's going to be a good season," said Daniela.

"A *great* season," said Kennedy.

"I like the sound of that," said Rinad.

They walked off the field together, arms still linked.

GRIDIRON

GRIDIRON
THE CLUTCH
PAUL HOBLIN

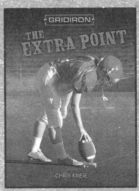

GRIDIRON
THE EXTRA POINT
CHRIS KREIE

GRIDIRON
FALSE START
PAUL HOBLIN

GRIDIRON
THE LATE HIT
K. R. COLEMAN

GRIDIRON
SHOWDOWN
K. R. COLEMAN

GRIDIRON
SIGNING DAY
K. R. COLEMAN

Leave it all on the field!

bOUnCE

bOUnCE
AT THE
CENTER
PATRICK JONES

bOUnCE
ON
GUARD
PATRICK JONES

bOUnCE
PASS IT
FORWARD
PATRICK JONES

bOUnCE
TO THE
POINT
PATRICK JONES

STEP UP YOUR GAME

ABOUT THE AUTHOR

Chris Kreie is an elementary school teacher in Eden Prairie, Minnesota. He's an avid sports fan and outdoorsman who especially enjoys hiking and camping near Lake Superior along Minnesota's north shore. He lives in Minneapolis with his wife and two children.